The Agent
of
GOLD

The Magic Telephone Booth 3

Kenny Ramos

Contents

This Book is dedicated to my bestest friend ever who I consider as my family because he has been with me through thick and thin and has made my life so much happier and I also helped him have a better life and I wouldn't have it anyother way.

CHAPTER I
The Play

Kenny, Tommy, and their family got invited to go see Cinderella on Broadway. "Awesome eeec I can't believe we're going to see my favorite fairy tale in the whole entire world," said Una. "I know it's exciting Una, but you, Tommy and I must go to Easton first. Then we will all meet at the location of the play," said Kenny. Tommy said, "Bro it's not safe we don't even know what will happen this time. Last time we went to the booth we almost died. Who knows what will happen on trip number three? We should go to the musical with mom and dad that way we don't get punished for changing a few fairy tale words." "What are you talking about Tommy? Please don't tell me that it was one of you and Kenny's dreams again," said Una.

"Uh sis, what Tommy is saying is completely true, but we have to take you there to believe us. Mom and Dad can me and Tommy go do that first?" said Kenny. "Yes son, but make sure you guys get to the play on time," said their dad. "Alright let's go," said Una. Kenny, Tommy and Una left. They went inside Tommy's car, and they all traveled to Easton.

* * *

Kenny, Tommy and their sister walked away from their car until they got to the telephone booth. "Well Una, this is the magical booth we've been talking about. First we need to go in and make a call to the backstage company for Broadway shows," said Kenny. "Alright, well Kenny and Tommy show me how it's done," said Una. Kenny, Tommy and Una all squeezed into the booth. Kenny went ahead and called the Broadway backstage company. Like their first two trips, the telephone booth called another number. The voice on the other side said, "If you want to go to the play press eight, if you want to go to the water park press two, if you want to call UPS press four, if you want to get ice cream press nine, and if you want to call the Backstage Pass company for Broadway press zero." "Ooo I want Ice cream let me press the number please guys," said Una. "Alright sis go right ahead," said Tommy. Una pressed the number seven by accident instead of nine and the ground started to shake.

The telephone booth went up and disappeared once again after five seconds.

CHAPTER 2
Arrested

*K*enny, Tommy and Una exited the booth which landed in a truck. They all walked out and stopped at a water station for some water. By the time they started walking again, Kenny, Tommy, and Una were stopped by the FBI. "You're under arrest for stealing and pushing the prince away," stated one of the members in the FBI. "Stop I'm only a fourteen year old I can't go to jail," said Una. The member of the FBI said, "Sorry ma'am you have to come with us." "Una run, make an army to help save us later, we'll be okay," said Tommy. Una listened.

She ran as fast as she could, but the driver of the FBI stopped her. Una was caught and arrested on the spot. Kenny and Tommy tried to run too, but the FBI arrested them before they could escape. The FBI drove Kenny and Tommy to their base. "Alright guys follow me to your rooms tonight," said the employee of the FBI. Kenny, Tommy, and Una followed the employee all the way to their rooms. "Okay Kenny your room is five, Tommy you get lucky number eight and Una yours is the first one next to me. Now that you know, go there and wait for instructions. See you all at the trial," said the employee. Tommy walked until he got to his room and he knocked.

"Who's there?" asked the voice. "Hello! I'm one of the people being trialed," said Tommy. The voice said, "Oh sweet, take off your shoes, leave them outside and come inside." "Okay I'm comin in," said Tommy. When he went in the person said, "Thank you for corporation. Go ahead and change then go to bed."

Tommy did exactly what he asked and then he fell asleep. The next Day Tommy woke up, went outside the room and noticed his favorite Jordan's were gone, but in their place was convict shoes. So Tommy put them on and then the employee came and said, "Awesome you're up and ready come on your siblings are waiting at the trial. I see that you snuck out to steal some shoes last night. Now this adds to the proof, get ready to be guilty." The employee took Tommy to the trial, and then they both sat down in their appropriate spots. The judge called the court to order and the trial began.

CHAPTER 3
The Trial

*K*enny, Tommy and Una were scared, they didn't know what was going to happen. "I'd like to call the defendants to the stand," said one of the agents. Kenny, Tommy and Una stood up, and walked to the stand. "Why in the world did you change a classic tale?" asked the prosecutor. "Well we changed it for our sister, because it was a tragic fate and she only knew of the Disney version," answered Kenny.

"Why did you make the prince of Ketchup marry a mermaid?" said the prosecutor. "We had the prince of Ketchup, formally known as Ivan marry the mermaid, because the prince was in love and he chose that path," answered Tommy. "Why are you here?" "Well I'm here, because I didn't believe my brothers stories, and they're not guilty of anything so please let us go," answered Una. The prosecutor said, "Well little girly that's where you're wrong your brother Tommy stole shoes which makes all of you guilty!"

The judge said, "Order in the court, look prosecutor you can't mark them guilty we do that. Alright everyone let's take a five minute break, and when we come back we'll state the result of the trial."

Five minutes later

"Alright order in the court. My trusted employee whats your plead on the defendants, innocent or guilty?" said the judge. The employee answered, "My most trusted friend the court and I find the defendants Guilty."

The judge said, "Guilty! Court dismissed. Defendants go to jail cell five in section D and wait for your deaths." Una said,

"Oh no! This can't be happening, I want to go home. Kenny... Tommy... What are we going do?"

CHAPTER 4
The Hanger

"*U*na I know what we'll do, we follow their orders it won't be that bad," said Kenny. Una said, "But, Kenny they said we are going to die." "No we won't follow me," said Kenny. Kenny, Tommy and Una all walked through section A, B, and C, but when they got to section D it was locked.

"Access code, please or no entrance," ordered the door keeper. "We don't know the code sir we're sorry, but we need to get to cell number five," answered Una. The door keeper said, "Well then I have to send you to floor two, room sixteen where you will die!" Five, four, three, two one... Before the siblings eyes a small door opened beneath them and they all fell through.

"Ahh! Help," yelled the siblings. Kenny, Tommy and Una arrived at floor two and they signed in. "Take a right, a left and then knock on door sixteen where you'll get orders," said the door keeper. Kenny, Tommy and Una walked then they took a right turn.

Once the siblings took their last turn they ended up at the wrong door. The siblings enter and find themselves at a plane. "Wow whats a plane doing in a jail cell," said Una. "Una we have something to tell you, this is our library disguised as a plane," answered Tommy.

"So that means we're not in a jail cell, but exactly what do they call this room," stated Una. Kenny answered, "We are in one of the county's airport hangers, and once we get inside the library be careful you don't ask for anything."

"Why?" asked Una.

"Sis, we know that something bad will happen so don't ask," said Tommy. "Okay let's go in," said Una. "Cool we agree," said Kenny.

CHAPTER 5
The Truth

*K*enny, Tommy and Una enter the plane. "Wow there's so many books where did you get it?" asked Una. "Someone put it there for us. We have to be careful that we don't touch the special ones because those are only to be opened on special occasions," said Kenny. "Ok. Too bad there isn't a book here for me to read. I truly wish someone could find a book for me," said Una.

A book came flying from a pile across the room and landed next to Una. Una picked up the book and said, "Wow I can't believe theres a book on secret agents. I love secret agents I wish I could see some for real." "No! Una why did you do that? You have no idea what's going to happen," said Tommy. Una said, "I saw this book and...

The engine started to roar. "Woah what was that?" asked Una. Kenny said, "Una you just gave our time machine a reason to move." All the siblings saw they were next to a car filled with secret agents.

The engine of the plane picked up and it began to fly. It flew faster and faster then everything was still absolutely still. "Cool that was fun let's do it again," said Una. "No we had enough excitement for today we should explore," said Tommy.

"I agree let's go," said Kenny.

CHAPTER 6
Captured

*B*y the time the siblings got up the secret agents walked up to the plane and they said, "Trespassers exit the plane immediately or else." Kenny said, "Una and Tommy go outside and I'll stay behind for a bit." Tommy and Una followed Kenny's instructions and they went outside the plane. Kenny quickly grabbed the research book notepad and pencil in a bag to successfully complete their trip. Kenny went out of the plane and the secret agents arrested the three siblings on the spot. "Not again. Now how are we going to get out of this one?" said Tommy. "Well I think we should follow their lead," said Una.

"Hey where are you taking us?" asked Kenny. "We are taking all of you to our secret command base," said the agents. On the way to their base the agents said, "Leave all communications here in the van and take everything else." The siblings left all their phones and Kenny kept his bag. The secret agents escorted Kenny, Tommy and Una out the van toward their base. By the time they were inside the secret agents took Una away as a slave. At that point the siblings knew they were captured.

CHAPTER 7
Dead Meat

They escorted Kenny and Tommy to their room. "Knock and wait for instructions," said one of the agents. Kenny knocked and the door keeper said, "Enter." Kenny entered and Tommy stayed behind. "Give me your shoes or you lose everything," said the room keeper.

Kenny said, "No leave me alone you creep." The door keeper got mad and ripped all Kenny's clothes except the shoes and gave Kenny a bathrobe to put on. Kenny wanted everything back, but the door keeper didn't return anything. "Leave your shoes here and take off your socks to save your brother," said the secret agent. Tommy did just that and a big guy took everything he had.

Tommy was dead meat now he knew whoever was behind the journeys failed to save him and his beloved siblings.

CHAPTER 8
Magical Escape

*K*enny sat down and opened the research book to a page with a secret agent holding a mysterious card. He read the caption below it out loud:

In all the years of the brutal secret agent book, there was always one that would betray the rest. His name was Secret agent Gold, and his purpose was to save those who would get trapped by the secret agent groups rules. The way you conjure or call Agent Gold is by an ancient spell made by his followers. The spell was:

"This man is good as gold, but don't be greedy when he tries to save you because you could be lost forever."

Kenny forgot to read the fine print, and five seconds after he read it there was a knock at the door. "Who's there," said the room keeper. "I'm the prosecutor and I'm here to assassinate the trespassers," said Secret agent Gold. "Oh come in," said the room keeper.

When Agent Gold came in he said, "Be Gone!" The room keeper vanished in a flash never to be seen again. "Now it's time for your death," said Agent Gold to Kenny. Kenny was so scared he said, "Please don't kill me and my brother, Please, Please, Please...

"Oh that was just a disguise, to make sure you were the one that didn't read the fine print and to get that bad guy away," said Agent Gold while interrupting Kenny's outrageous fright. "Oops I'm sorry I'll do that next time, but how do we get our clothes back before we escape?" said Kenny.

"Well that's a great question, and the answer to it is in your book," said Agent Gold. Kenny asked, "Cool, what page do I turn to?"

Mr. Gold answered, "Turn to page 50, and you will see a basket of lost in a picture on the beach. All you have to do is read the spell and all will be fixed." Kenny reopened the Secret Agent book, and he flipped through it until he got to page fifty. He read the caption out loud:

The Secret Agent group always had a way of ripping people's clothes, when they don't listen. All the persons items don't go to the trash, they all are reconstructed and land on a mysterious beach. The only way to summon the items is to enchant the groups betrayer to recite a quick summoning spell. The special spell is:

"Agent Gold is here to serve, help him finish his job by bringing lost treasures back in a flash."

After Kenny read the spell Mr. Gold said, "Basket Basket come to me now." The basket with Kenny and Tommy's clothes appeared in a flash. Kenny quickly changed back into his normal clothes and after that Tommy showed up.

"Tommy quick switch out your robe for your regular clothes," said Kenny. "What about our shoes?" asked Tommy. "Worry about that later just change quickly and please hurry," answered Kenny.

Tommy listened and changed from the robe he had back to normal clothes in five seconds straight. "Now how do we get back to the plane and save Una at the same time?" asked

Tommy. "Sweet, now we're talking my deed. To answer your question you must read one more spell before I give you this," said Agent Gold as he held up a gold key card.

Kenny said, "Alright then where can we find it, Mr. Gold?" "You can find this on the final page of your research book," said Agent Gold. Kenny gave the book to Tommy and said, "Tommy open the book and flip to the last page to read the final spell. Please hurry we don't have much time."

Tommy knew exactly what to do. First he opened the book, next he flipped through every page until he found a picture with two pairs of lost Jordans in a grocery store.

He read the caption out loud:

The Secret Agent group had a secret organization working with them. The organization would always find a way to find their prisoners guilty as charged. Most of the helpers would steal their prisoners shoes just so that they could lose. The only way to return the stolen shoes was to have Mr. Gold A.K.A. Agent Gold to say a finding spell before he left. The spell during that day was:

"There isn't much time left for Mr. Gold, make the finding spell very speedy so we can leave in a hurry."

After Tommy read the spell he said, "Sorry guys after the spell I'll be gone, but take this card as my little gratitude for helping me with my duty's. Time is running out so make their shoes run like the wind all the way to them." Kenny's and Tommy's Jordans appeared in a flash and they put them on right away. Before Kenny and Tommy could thank Mr. Gold, he vanished only to be seen by hsi next ruler.

In Mr. Gold's place was an arrow pointing towards a golden double door. "Kenny look a gold door I believe it's our way out, let's go," said Tommy. Kenny said, "I agree bro lets get out of here."

Kenny and Tommy walked all the way to the golden double doors, and they inserted the golden key card where it said: **Enter Card here***

The doors opened and they figured out it was a secret elevator made by Agent Gold for emergencies only. Before the elevators, double doors closed someone said, "Yes you guys are alive I knew the elevator was magic when I escaped from those agent creeps." "Una we're so glad you're okay!" said Tommy with excitement. "Where's the time machine?" asked Kenny. "It's on the ground floor, and we're almost there," said Una. "Oh no! I forgot the bag with all our items in it," said Kenny while sounding worried. "Don't worry Una has it," said Tommy with nourishment.

"Yes I do! Sorry I didn't tell you earlier I had to make sure they didn't change you guys in any way. Awesome we're here," said Una. The elevator doors opened and the silings walked out until they arrived at the plane. "Who's ready to go to the musical?" asked Tommy. "We are," said Kenny and Una at the same time. "Cool lets all get in the plane and find the book on the telephone booth," said Tommy. The siblings entered the plane, they all sat down and Una closed the doors for the first time.

CHAPTER 9
Back to the Future

"Hey guys how do we get back home?" asked Una. Tommy answered, "Oh sis that's easy first we need to find the book on the telephone booth and then make a wish to get back. Finally we make a call home and chose where we want to go. After that we will finally be reunited with mom and dad at the musical." "Sweet so can one of you demonstrate for me, since it's my first time and I'm still new at the whole wishing things up phenomenon," said Una. Kenny said, "Una I would gladly be happy in showing you how to get home. Tommy quick find the book on the telephone booth." "Sure thing bro," said Tommy.

Tommy searched every single pile until he saw a red book with a huge 'B' on the front. Tommy said, "Kenny I found the book, but it looks different is that okay?" Kenny said, "Yes just open it to a random page and give it to me." Tommy opened the book to a random page and said, "Here you go," while handing it to his brother. Kenny pointed to a picture with a red box inside it and Kenny said, "I wish we could go there."

Una noticed they were next to a bush with the telephone booth and she said, "Now I understand. I'm so sorry for getting us into this mess. Can you forgive me?" Tommy answered, "Yes it's okay, next time you can come with us, because it's obvious you learned your lesson." "So you guys knew I..." The engine of the plane began to roar and the wind picked up. The propellor of the plane started and it began to fly.

The plane flew faster and faster than everything was still absolutely still. Kenny looked at the time and said, "Una we all have to call mom and dad to let them know we might be late for the play." "Ok I'm ready let's go," said Una. Kenny, Tommy and Una exited the plane and walked all the way to the booth. All of the silings entered the booth to phone home.

CHAPTER 10
Just in Time

"*K*enny can I call mom and dad because its my fault we'll be late," said Una. Kenny said, "Yes go right ahead, but make it quick because I truly don't like tight spaces." Una said, "I'll try my best."

Una made a quick phone call home and the booth decided to call another number. The voice message came on and said, "Hello if you need to speak with your parents press 1 now, if you want to go to a concert press 4, if you want to enter a race press 7 and, if you want to get to a musical press 2." Una quickly pressed two and seven then the booth vanished into thin air.

* * *

The telephone booth landed right in front of the the theatre where the play was showing. All the siblings exited the booth, saw their parents and said, "Mm. Dad. Wait for us we're coming." Kenny said, "Look guys there's a huge **B** on the doors of the booth." "You know what that means, the booth belongs to the **B** person," said Tommy. "Let's get to mom and dad before we lose them," said Una. "I agree let's go," said Kenny. All of the siblings ran to their parents, and just in time they reunited with them before they scanned their tickets. The whole family sat down and began to watch *Cinderella the Musical.*

www.ingramcontent.com/pod-product-compliance
Lightning Source LLC
Chambersburg PA
CBHW050900130726
47900CB00013B/761